ESCAPE
from the
CHANTICLEER

Hope you have as much fun reading this tale as I had illustrating it.

Barbara van Winckelen.

Dedicated to
children
of all
ages.

Published in the United States by Winds & Dragons, Inc.

Printed in China

Library of Congress Catalog Card Number: 95-90348

ISBN: 0-9646819-0-0

Printed on recycled paper.

ESCAPE
from the
CHANTICLEER

Illustrations by Barbara van Winkelen
Story by Jared Tausig & Eva-Maria Tausig

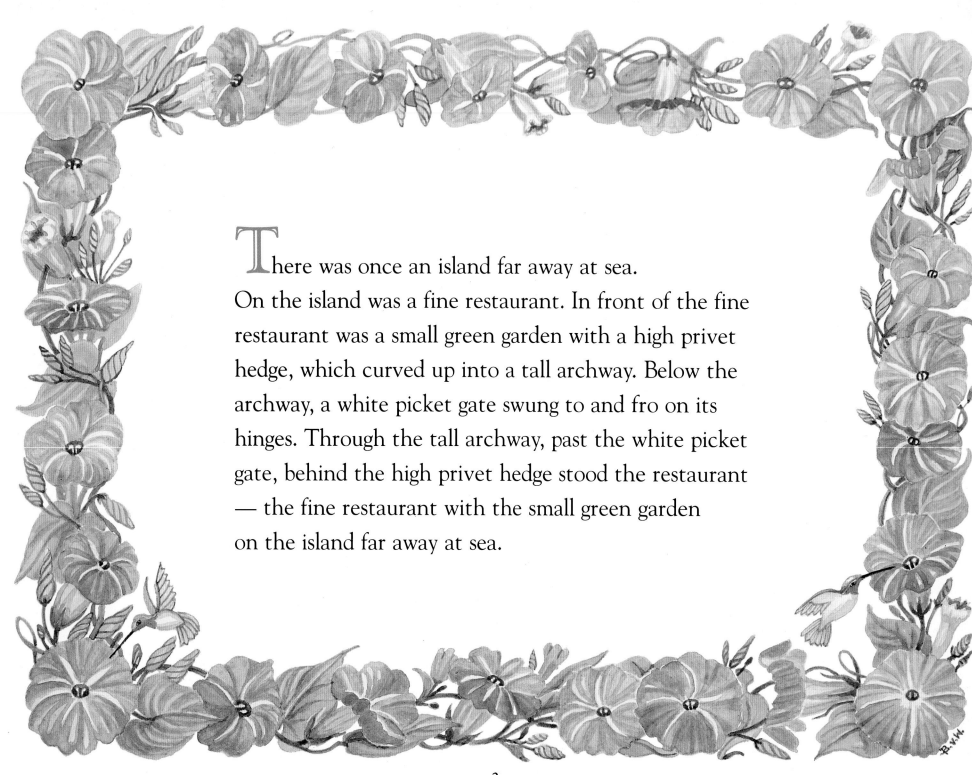

There was once an island far away at sea.
On the island was a fine restaurant. In front of the fine restaurant was a small green garden with a high privet hedge, which curved up into a tall archway. Below the archway, a white picket gate swung to and fro on its hinges. Through the tall archway, past the white picket gate, behind the high privet hedge stood the restaurant — the fine restaurant with the small green garden on the island far away at sea.

On top of the grey-shingled roof of the restaurant perched a proud French rooster. The proud French rooster looked over the small green garden towards the high privet hedge. The fine restaurant took its name from this weathervane.

Rooster in French is *Chanticleer*, and Chanticleer was the name of the restaurant with the small green garden on the island far away at sea.

In the center of the small green garden was a merry-go-round horse. Flowers danced at his feet when the wind blew. In the morning, the sun felt warm on his back; at night, the fog was pleasant and cool. There he stood, silently watching and listening to the people who came to eat at the Chanticleer.

Early one evening, a girl with a long ponytail and her little brother came to the Chanticleer for dinner. While they were waiting, they played in the small green garden. The girl looked at the flowers, and the boy stood on his tiptoes to pat the merry-go-round horse on the nose. The merry-go-round horse listened to the girl and her little brother as they talked.

The two children talked about going to the beach with their parents. Running on the sand, the children would play tag with the waves. Darting as close to the water as they dared, they would run laughing and shouting up the beach as the waves came leaping to catch them. Sometimes, the waves were faster, and the foamy, white fingers of the sea made their feet wet. Swimming and playing in the water, they loved to feel the spray of the ocean. It left a salty taste on their lips.

They even built a sand castle, decorating it with some of the
treasures they found. When they got tired they wrapped
themselves in fluffy towels, climbed the dunes, sat in the warm
sand and watched the sea. Their eyes sparkled as they talked
about the day at the beach, while they stood in the small green
garden at the front of the fine restaurant.

The girl with the long ponytail and her little brother loved to go and swing on the swings. At the beach, four black rubber swings hung on chains from a pipe. The children would swing back and forth. Every time they pumped with their legs, they went a little bit higher. When they swung forward, they would look far out to sea and watch the sailboats of the rainbow fleet racing the wind. When they swung back, they would look down between their toes and see the white tops of the Queen Anne's Lace and the pink petals of the beach roses bobbing in the breeze.

They would swing, until they were almost as high as the bar itself. So high that they fancied they were higher than the tall lighthouse — the tall white lighthouse with the black top and the red stripe around its middle. The tall lighthouse stood on a high bluff far up the beach. At night, the bright beam of the lighthouse would slowly spin round and round, so all the boats could find the far away island.

The merry-go-round horse had been listening closely as the girl with the long ponytail and her little brother talked. He heard about running on the sand, playing tag with the waves, and the lighthouse shining so brightly at night. He heard, and he was sad.

He wanted to run on the sand, play tag with the waves, feel the spray of the ocean on his face, and look far out to sea. All he ever saw was the inside of the small green garden, the proud French rooster, and the people who came to eat at the Chanticleer — the fine restaurant on the island far away at sea.

After finishing dessert, the girl and her little brother followed their parents back through the garden, towards the white picket gate below the tall archway in the high hedge. The boy stopped and came back to pat the merry-go-round horse on the nose, and then hurried to catch up with his family as they left the small green garden. The merry-go-round horse watched the gate swing shut and dreamt about doing everything the children had talked about — running on the sand, playing tag with the waves, and feeling the spray of the ocean on his face.

If only he could leave the green garden. If only he could pass the white gate. If only he could escape for a little while …

17

That night — when all was quiet and still, after all the people
left the Chanticleer and went to bed, after the rooster closed his
eyes to sleep, and after the yellow moon rose softly — the merry-
go-round horse began to stir. Carefully, he picked his way around
the flowers that danced at his feet. He pushed his way past the
white picket gate, through the tall archway in the high privet
hedge, out of the small green garden and onto the streets of the
little town on the island far away at sea.

Once beyond the garden, the horse began to trot, then canter, and finally gallop as fast as his white legs could carry him. His black-painted hooves clicked on the brick sidewalk as he trotted by the weather-beaten houses. His hooves clattered on the stones of the narrow cobbled path as he cantered down the bluff. Then they thundered on the wooden planks as he galloped toward the sea.

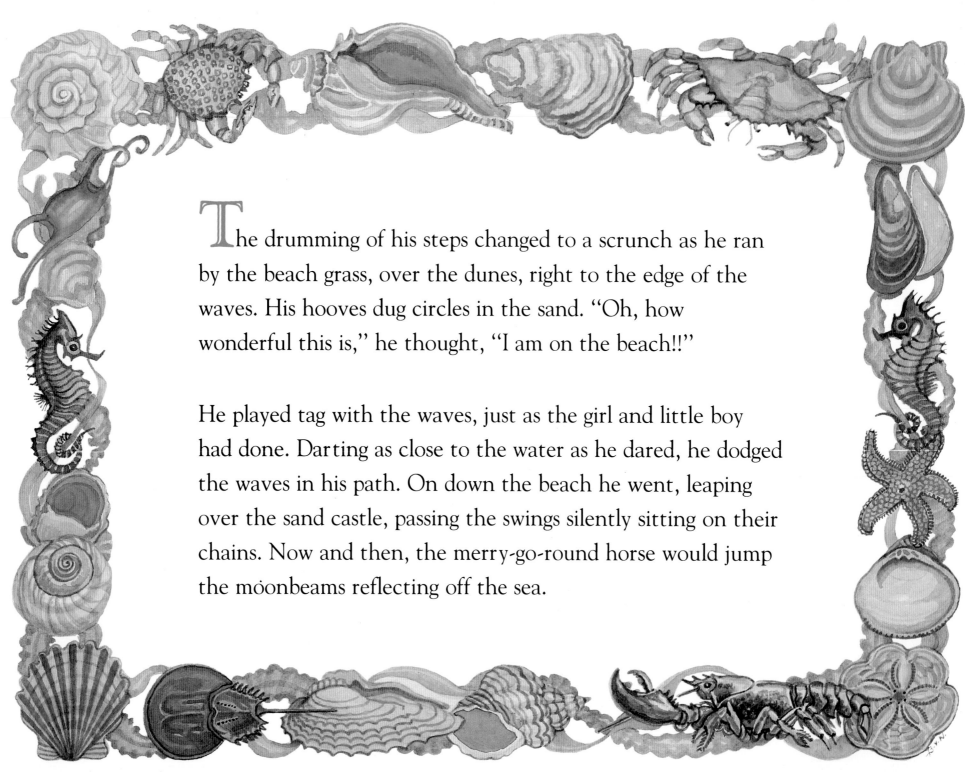

The drumming of his steps changed to a scrunch as he ran by the beach grass, over the dunes, right to the edge of the waves. His hooves dug circles in the sand. "Oh, how wonderful this is," he thought, "I am on the beach!!"

He played tag with the waves, just as the girl and little boy had done. Darting as close to the water as he dared, he dodged the waves in his path. On down the beach he went, leaping over the sand castle, passing the swings silently sitting on their chains. Now and then, the merry-go-round horse would jump the moonbeams reflecting off the sea.

22

He stopped, quite out of breath, and turned around to follow his tracks back up the beach. In the distance, he saw the bright beam of the tall lighthouse. The merry-go-round horse was happy, and he began running again, faster and faster. And so he sped, zigging and zagging, leaping and jumping, seeming to float over the sand.

What a glorious feeling to be free, with the wind in his mane, the sand under his hooves, and the spray of the ocean in his face. As he ran, the moon sank lower and lower in the night sky. The merry-go-round horse knew it was time to go back to the small green garden. He left the swings and the beach behind. He cantered over the sandy dunes, past the beach grass, and trotted gingerly up the cobbled path.

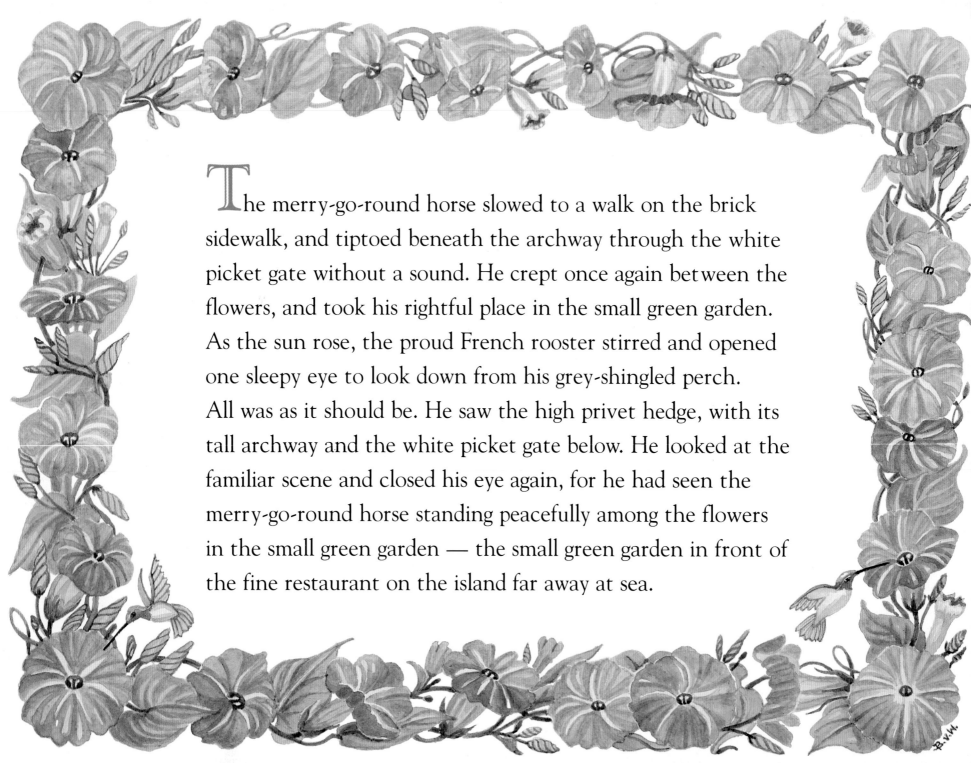

The merry-go-round horse slowed to a walk on the brick sidewalk, and tiptoed beneath the archway through the white picket gate without a sound. He crept once again between the flowers, and took his rightful place in the small green garden. As the sun rose, the proud French rooster stirred and opened one sleepy eye to look down from his grey-shingled perch. All was as it should be. He saw the high privet hedge, with its tall archway and the white picket gate below. He looked at the familiar scene and closed his eye again, for he had seen the merry-go-round horse standing peacefully among the flowers in the small green garden — the small green garden in front of the fine restaurant on the island far away at sea.

Barbara is a graduate of the Yale University School of Fine Art. For 18 summers she has painted at Spindrift, her Old South Wharf Studio-Gallery on Nantucket, the island far away at sea. Her Maine Coon cat, Häagen, modeled for some illustrations in this book.

Born in New York, **Jared** currently lives in Massachusetts with his wife Heather. He represents at least six generations of storytellers. He has enjoyed Nantucket his entire life, and has spent countless hours watching the ocean while riding each of the four swings.

Eva-Maria remembers her own childhood summers — having daily breakfasts, lunches, and dinners at the Chanticleer, when that was usual. Her four children thrived on the island, sharing her with Nantucket's Musical Arts Society, the Chamber Music Center, the Garden Club, the Artists' Association, among other activities.